Mack's Made-Up Stories

by Kelli Port
illustrated by Mary Sullivan

SCHOLASTIC INC.

New York • Toronto • London • Auckland
Sydney • Mexico City • New Delhi • Hong Kong

No part of this publication may be reproduced, stored in a retrieval system, or transmitted in any form or by any means, electronic, mechanical, photocopying, recording, or otherwise, without written permission of the publisher. For information regarding permission, write to Scholastic Inc., Attention: Permissions Department, 557 Broadway, New York, NY 10012.

ISBN 978-0-545-68604-4

Copyright © 2010 by Lefty's Editorial Services.
All rights reserved. Published by Scholastic Inc.
SCHOLASTIC, LET'S LEARN READERS™, and associated logos
are trademarks and/or registered trademarks of Scholastic Inc.

12 11 10 9 8 7 6 5 4 3 2   14 15 16 17 18 19/0

Printed in China.

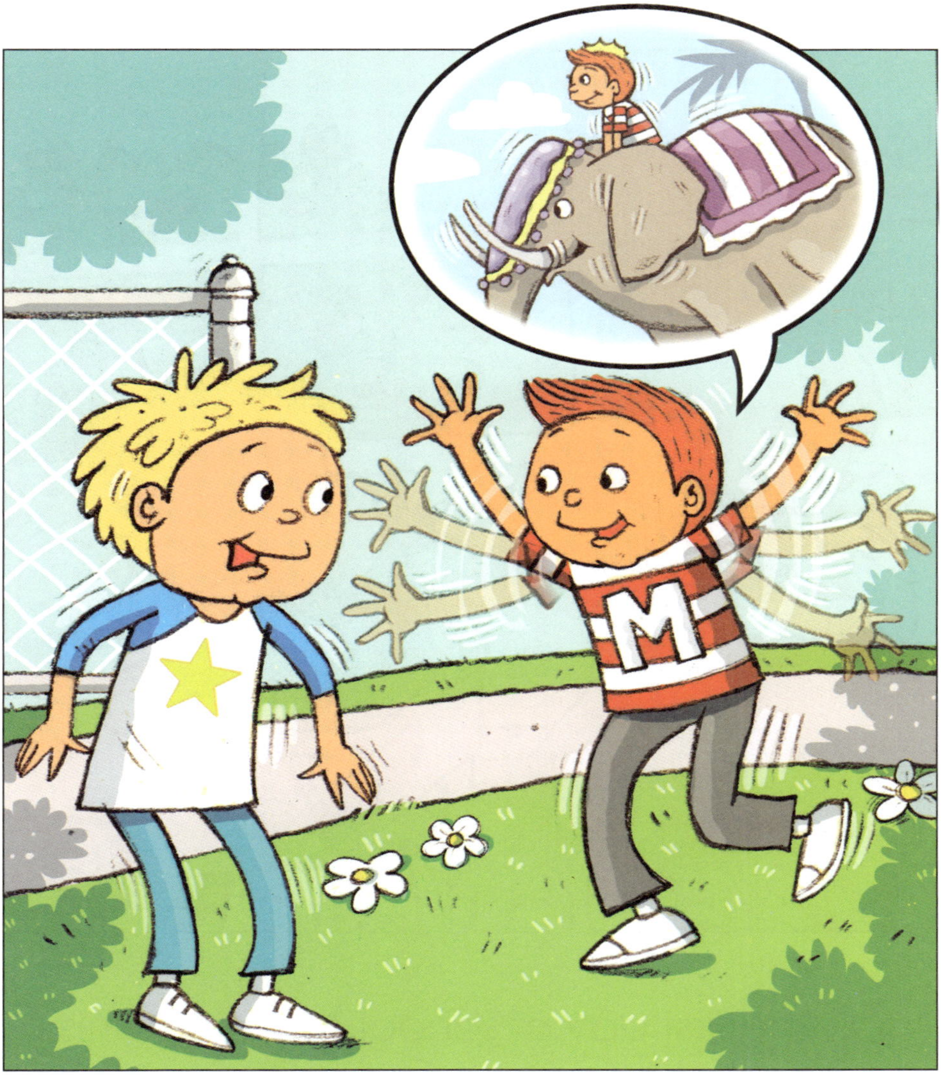

Mack loved telling kids about his adventures! There was only one problem: Sometimes he made things up.

 **Why might it be a problem for Mack to make things up?**

On the first day of school, Mack saw his friend Sara.

"I had the best summer vacation," said Mack.

"What did you do?" asked Sara.

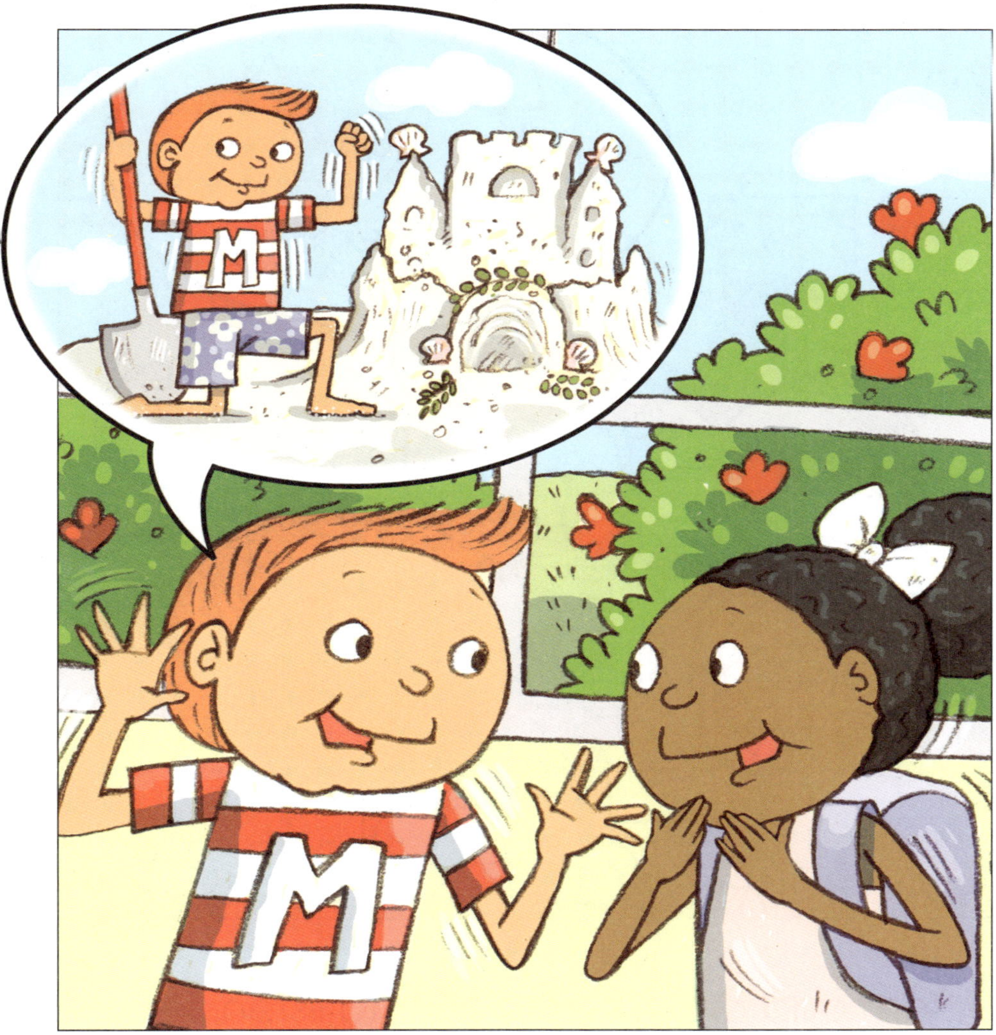

"My family went to the beach. I built a huge sandcastle," said Mack.
That part was true.

 **Is Sara interested in Mack's story? How can you tell?**

Tom and Molly came over to listen.

"I was digging in the sand when my shovel hit something hard. It was a box," said Mack.

That part was true, too.

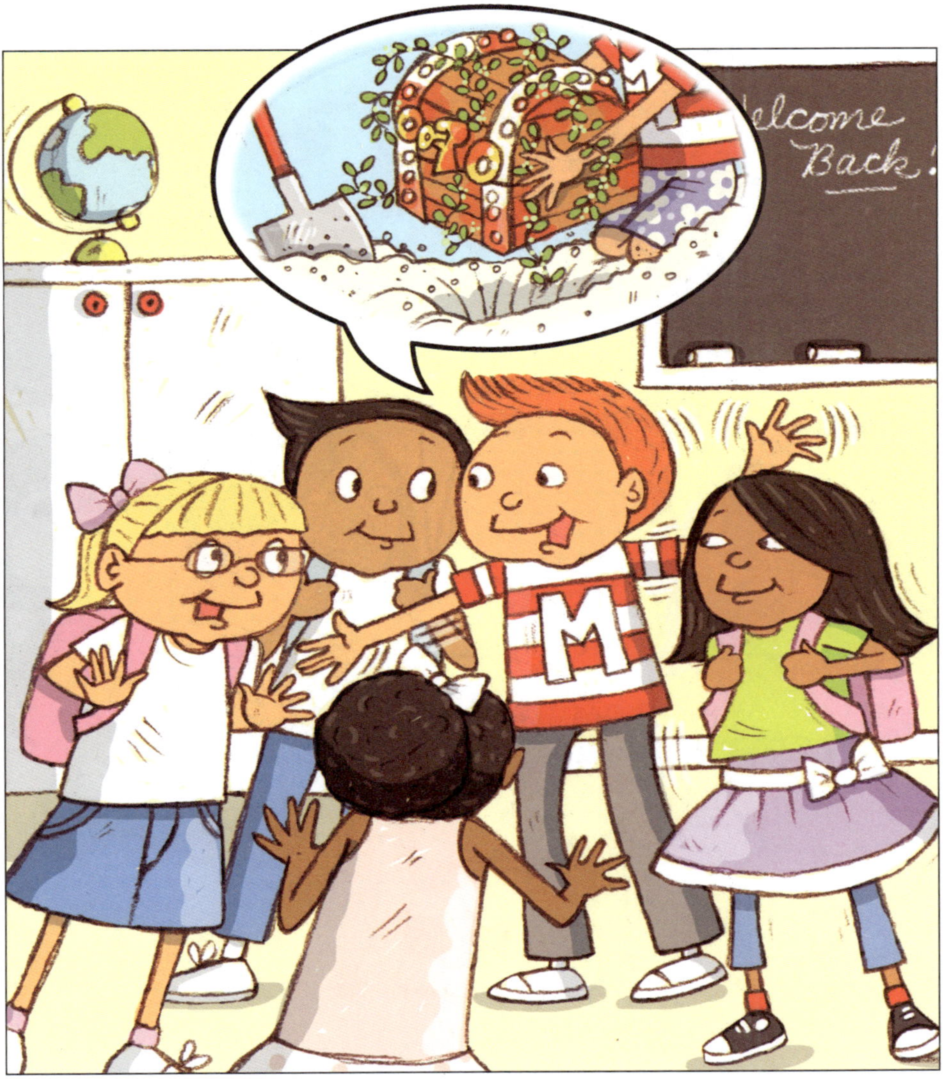

"The box was big and rusty and covered with seaweed," said Mack.
Uh-oh! That part was NOT true.

What do you think Mack will say is inside the box?

By now, a lot of kids were listening.

Mack went on, "When I opened the box, I could not believe my eyes. It was filled with fancy jewels and one hundred gold coins!"

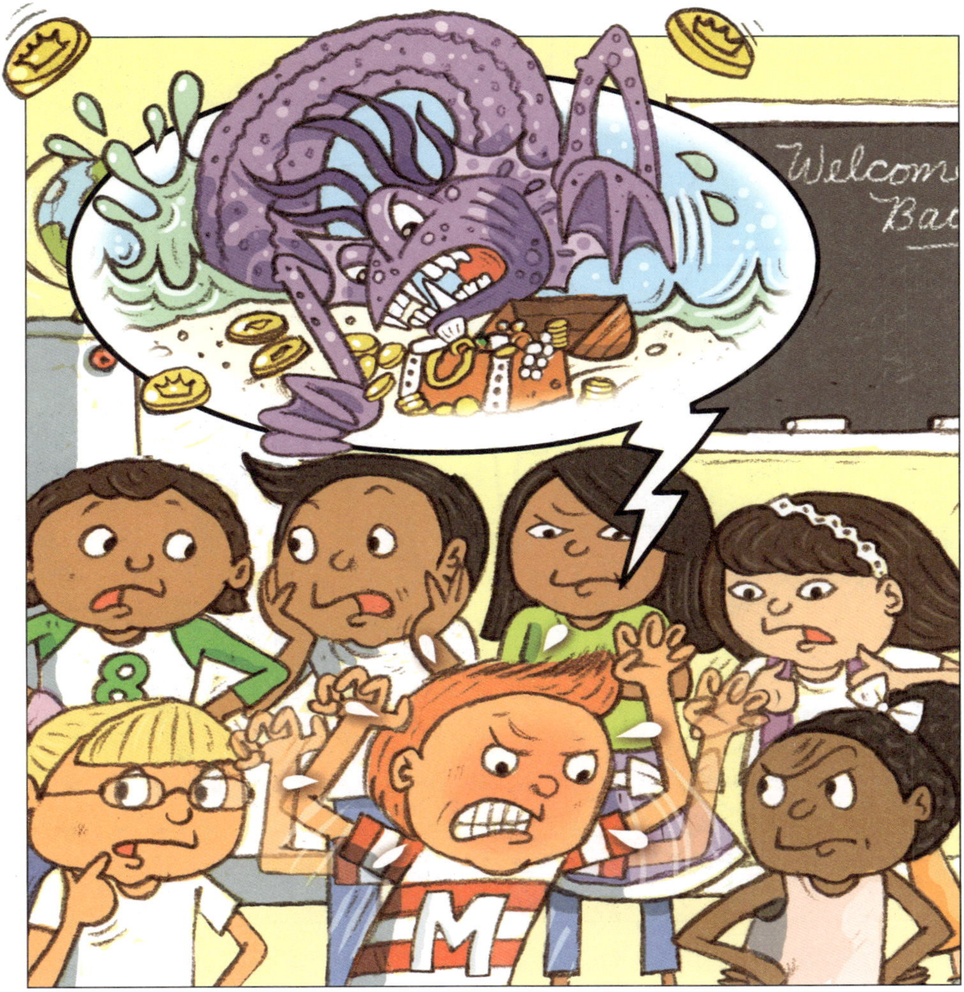

"Suddenly, a giant purple sea monster rose out of the water," said Mack. "The sea monster roared, 'Give me back my one thousand gold coins!'"

Do you think Mack is telling the truth? Why or why not?

"I thought you said there were *one hundred* coins," said Sara.

"There is no such thing as a sea monster," said Tom.

"You made that up!" said Molly.

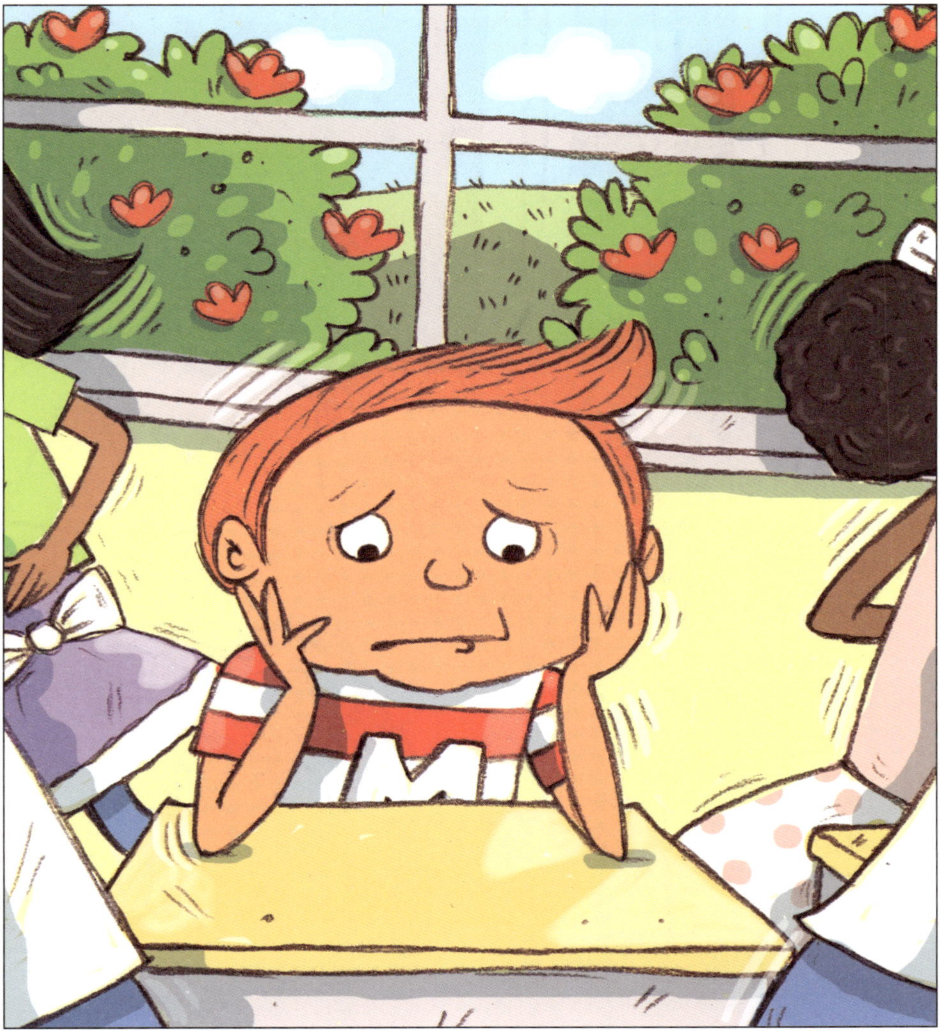

The kids walked away. Mack didn't mean to make things up. He just wanted the kids to listen to his adventure.

Why did the kids walk away? How do you think this made Mack feel?

The teacher, Mr. Moss, noticed Mack was upset.

"You have a great imagination," Mr. Moss said. "Why don't you use it to write a story?"

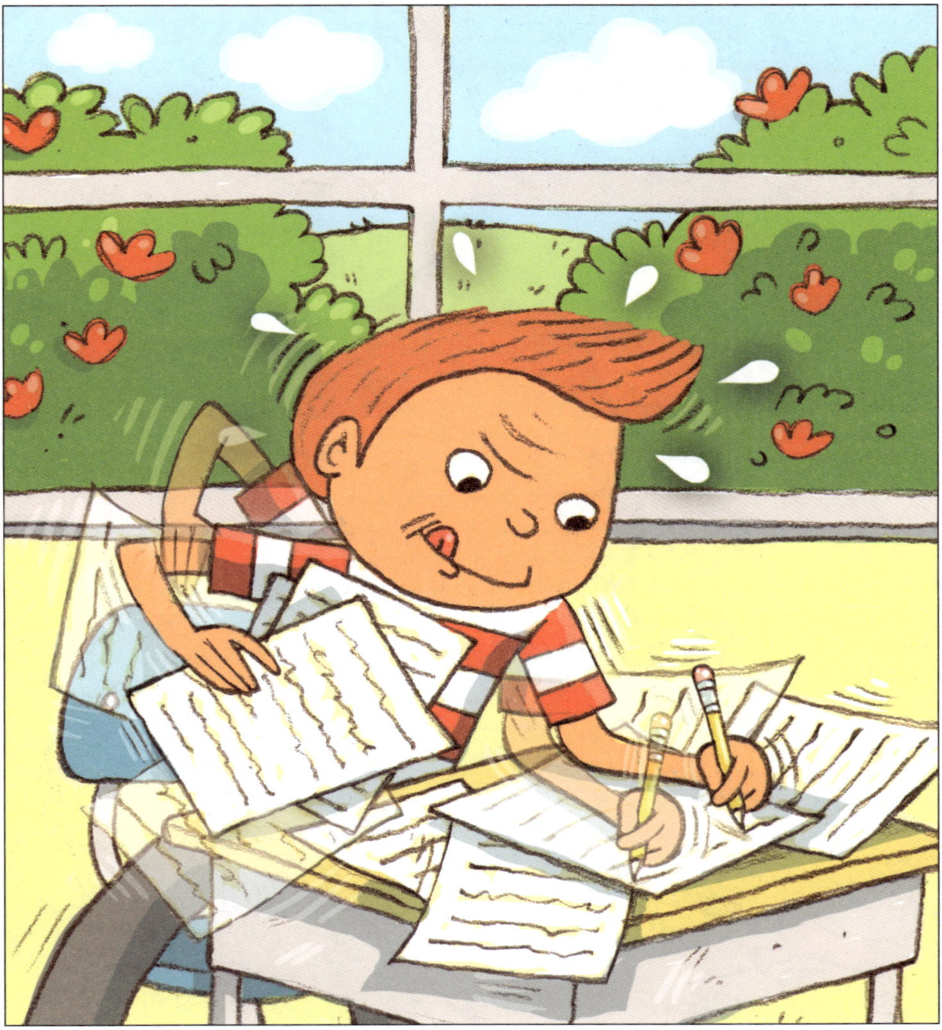

What a great idea! Mack took out his pencil and began writing and writing and writing. At last, his story was done.

Have you ever written a story? What was it about?

Mr. Moss asked Mack to read the story to the whole class. It had a giant and a king and gold coins and even a talking sea monster.

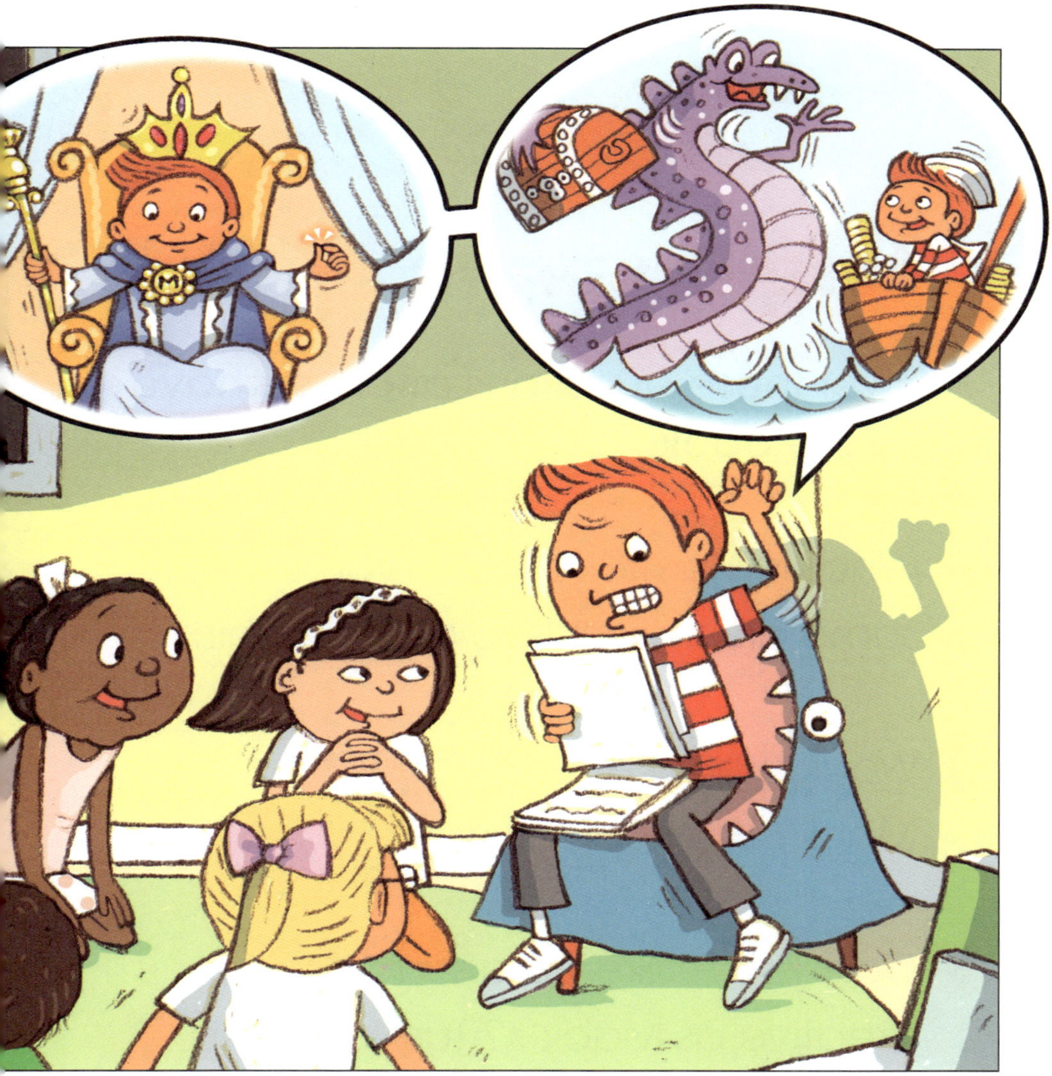

The kids loved Mack's story. And Mack loved finding a way to use his amazing imagination!

What lesson did Mack learn?

Story Prompts

Answer these questions after you have read the book.

1. What is Mack like? Can you think of some great words to describe him?

2. Would you like to be friends with Mack? Why or why not?

3. Can you make up a story as creative as Mack's? Turn on your imagination and give it a try!